Parents' Magazine Press • New York

THE
KITCHEN-WINDOW
SQUIRREL

by Harold Longman   pictures by Nola Langner

Most affectionately for Anne and George Popkin

"Well," said Dad, rubbing his hands to
warm them up and looking very pleased with
himself. "I'm all done. Now we can watch
the birds having their breakfast while we
have ours."
Davy looked out the kitchen window.
On the windowsill, easy to see, Dad had
built a narrow shelf. On it he had nailed
one of Mom's old pie pans.

The pan was full of birdseed.
"How will the birds know it's here?" asked
Davy.
"If it's food," said Dad, "the birds will
find it. And with winter almost here, they
won't have too many places to look."
"I can hardly wait," said Davy.
"You'll have to," said Dad.
"LOOK!" cried Davy.

A tiny bird swooped down, picked up a seed,
and flew off.
"Gosh!" said Davy. "He's pretty smart.
You know, that was the closest I ever saw a
wild bird."
"It's a chickadee," said Dad. "They're
very brave. Soon we will know all the
different kinds of birds that live here."

"This is a fine way to go bird-watching,"
said Davy, as he reached for another piece of
toast. "Will he be back?"
"He's gone to tell his friends," said Dad.
The chickadee did not come back that
morning. But next morning, Davy came to
breakfast very early and there were three
chickadees at the bird feeder. They were
almost close enough to touch.

When they saw Davy, they flew away.
Davy's mother came in to fix breakfast.
Davy said, "There were three chickadees at
the bird feeder. But they flew away when I
looked at them."
"They will come back," said his mother.
"They want their breakfast as much as you do.
Soon they will be used to you. Would you
like scrambled eggs?"

"All right," said Davy. "Are you sure?"
"Very sure," said his mother.
"Then may I have pancakes instead?"
"The birds are easier to feed," said
Davy's mother, smiling.
She was right about the chickadees.
They came back. Soon they were very
much at home. As the days grew colder, with
flurries of snow, other birds came, too.

There were a pair of juncos, gray as stone.
A grosbeak, splashed with color.
Two quarrelsome sparrows.
A cardinal, red as roses.
A tiny bunting, brown on top, white as a
snowflake below.
A tiny finch, like a sparrow dipped in
raspberry juice. And a little striped
woodpecker with a long, slender beak.

The birds looked at Davy with bright
little eyes, bold as you please.
The bigger birds drove the smaller birds
away until they were finished.
The smaller birds would sit patiently on
a branch of the oak tree near the window
and wait for their breakfast.
But all the birds ate as much as they
pleased.

One morning Davy was having breakfast
inside. Two juncos were having breakfast
outside.
Suddenly they scattered.
PLOP!
A squirrel, leaping from the oak like a
diver from a tower, landed smack in the
middle of the bird feeder.
Davy was so startled, he spilled his milk.

The squirrel looked at Davy with eyes like
shiny brown buttons. And he went right on
eating.
It was amazing to see how fast the
birdseed disappeared.
"He's scared all the birds away!" cried
Davy. "And he'll eat up all their food!"
"Tap on the window," said Davy's mother.
Davy tapped hard on the window.

With a quick twitch, the squirrel stood up,
ready to leap away. But he did not leap. He
simply stared at Davy, waiting. After a
moment, he started to eat again.
"Open the window," said Davy's mother.
Davy opened the window.
The squirrel leaped off the bird feeder
onto a branch and sat there waiting.
Davy didn't know what to do next.

"Close the window," said Davy's mother.
"It's cold."
Davy closed the window.
The squirrel leaped back into the bird
feeder and started to whoosh up birdseed all
over again.
Davy went outside and looked at the squirrel.
The squirrel looked at Davy. Davy had never
disliked an animal so much in all his life.

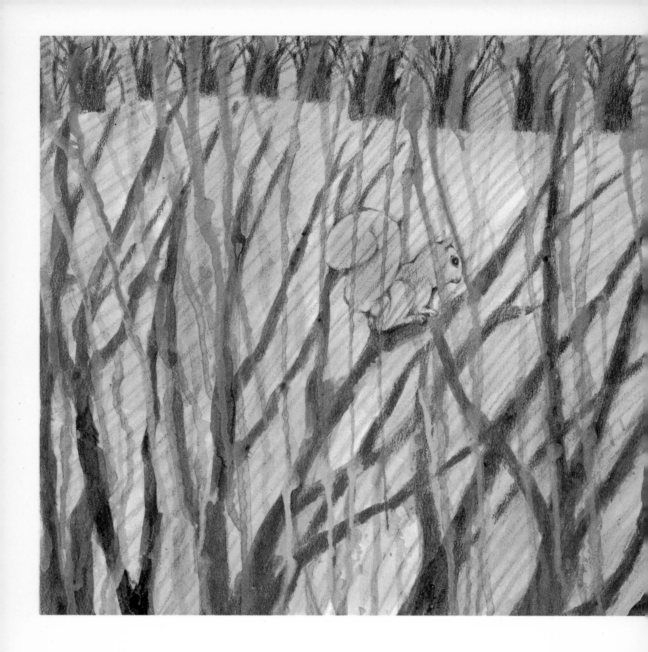

After that, the squirrel came back every
morning and started gobbling away.
Davy would open the window. The squirrel
would leap away. He would watch Davy from
his tree. As soon as the window was closed
he would leap back.
There was no getting rid of him.
And the birds had to wait and wait for
their breakfast.

There were days now when it rained.
Then the snow froze, hard as pavement,
and it seemed even colder.
Did the birds get enough food, Davy
wondered. His mother said they did,
but Davy worried about them.
And every morning the squirrel came,
fat and sleek in his warm winter coat,
bright-eyed and bold.

Davy tried throwing a glass of water at
the squirrel. But by the time he opened the
window and reached out to throw the water,
the squirrel was on his branch, just out of reach.
Sometimes Davy got a few drops of water
on the squirrel's tail. The squirrel just
shook out his tail and sat on his branch.
As soon as Davy turned his head, the squirrel
was back, whooshing away.

Davy took his whole week's allowance and
bought a plastic water pistol.
Next morning he waited for the squirrel,
his gun loaded.
PLOP!
The squirrel was in the bird feeder.
Davy squeezed the trigger.
With the window open only a crack, he
could not aim very well. He missed.

The squirrel went right on eating. Davy
was out of ammunition.
Dad was very much amused.
"That is one smart squirrel," he said. "He
almost deserves his breakfast."
Davy didn't think it was so funny.
"There has to be a way," he thought.
It was the squirrel or Davy.
But the squirrel seemed to be winning.

Davy put some of his mother's detergent
into his water pistol. "He won't like that,"
Davy thought.
He shot detergent at the squirrel. It
made a lovely stream of bubbles through the
air. The squirrel watched them with interest
from his branch.
Davy was sure the squirrel was laughing
at him.

Next morning, Davy took his air gun with
the rubber-tipped darts, and waited at the
window.
He felt like a sheriff in a western town,
waiting for a dangerous outlaw.
PLOP!
The squirrel was back.
POP! The gun made a terrible
noise in the early morning quiet.

The dart whizzed over the squirrel, almost
close enough to touch him.
The squirrel sat on his branch for a few
moments, chattering angrily.
Then, as Davy reached for another dart,
the squirrel scurried up the tree, out of
sight.
"I sure showed him," thought Davy.
But he wasn't very sure.

Sure enough, the squirrel did not come
back next morning.
Or the next.
Davy thought the squirrel had finally
learned his lesson.
"I guess I showed him," thought Davy.
Still, breakfast wasn't quite the same
when Davy didn't have the squirrel to shoo
away.

Davy thought of the squirrel's pointed
face and bright, brown eyes. He thought of
the way the squirrel had leaped onto a branch,
just out of reach. He thought of the way
the squirrel had leaped back when Davy
closed the window.
Sometimes the squirrel had almost missed
the branch. Then he had to scramble to
climb back.

Thinking about it, the squirrel seemed
quite funny to Davy. And very brave.
Even if he ate bird food, instead of
gathering nuts, as squirrels should.
Looking out the window—just in case
the squirrel might surprise him and come
back—Davy saw the first sign of green
buds on the bare branches.

The pale green swellings turned into tiny
leaves.
The birds came every morning.
Occasionally, a new bird would appear,
very shy at first. But soon he was quite at
home.
First there was a cowbird, glossy black,
with a brown head.

One morning a bluebird came, sky-blue,
with a little round, red breast.
Robins hopped around the lawn.
Davy watched them, pleased.
Yet it seemed strange that the squirrel
had not come back. Not even once. Davy
didn't know why he kept thinking of the
squirrel.

One fine afternoon, Davy didn't feel like
doing anything special.
He wandered around, wondering what he
wanted to do.
Then he thought, just for fun, he might
look for the squirrel.
It was something to do.

Davy climbed the tree near the kitchen
window. Nothing there. Not even a place
where a squirrel might live.
He climbed other trees. He didn't find
anything. He hadn't expected to.
"I guess he's moved away," thought Davy.
He told himself that he was glad.
But there was one tree that Davy had not
climbed, in the corner of the yard.

Davy's father had said he would cut that
tree down some day because it had so
many rotten branches.
"One last look," Davy told himself and he
swung himself up.
Then he saw a big knothole in the trunk of
another tree. Davy looked into the hole.
There was nothing to see. It was dark
inside.

Davy was about to climb down when he
thought he saw something move inside.
He began to feel excited.
He was sure now that he was looking into
a bright little pair of eyes.
It must be his squirrel!
The squirrel stayed quite still. Only
his eyes gleamed.
Then Davy gasped.

He was sure he saw something else in the
hole.
He leaned closer.
Yes!
There were two other little pairs of eyes.
They were hard to see because they were
closed, mostly. When they blinked they were
tiny and bright.
BABY SQUIRRELS!

Davy's squirrel wasn't a *he* at all!
Now Davy knew why she had not come to the
bird feeder.
Davy wished he had not shot that dart.
But he was glad he had missed.
He thought he might bring some birdseed
tomorrow.
Just then the squirrel, so still before,
started to chatter excitedly.

Startled, Davy grasped at a branch
overhead. As he did, the branch beneath his
foot cracked and fell to the ground.
Davy's feet swung in midair. He held on
tight, reaching for a foothold on the tree
trunk.
One foot found the squirrel hole. It
was just big enough for one foot, but it
was solid.

Davy put one arm around the tree trunk,
then the other.
He rested his weight on the knothole.
Now he tried to slide down, carefully.
He felt his jeans r-r-rip.
He was sliding faster than he wanted to.
Branches broke beneath his feet, slowing
him a little.

And he landed on the ground with a jolt.
He was scratched up a bit. His jeans were
torn. But he was safe.
He thought, "The squirrel tried to warn me.
She started to chatter just before the branch
broke."
He walked slowly toward the house,
thinking about how mean he had been.

The trees were in full leaf now.
The daffodils and the tulips had already
bloomed and faded. The weather was getting
warm.
The birds did not come to the window so
often; there were more interesting places
to look for food.
One morning Davy's mother was fixing breakfast.
PLOP!

Davy looked up.
His squirrel was back, eating away. Now
and then she would glance up. Not toward
Davy, but back toward the tree. On a branch,
two smaller squirrels sat watching her.
Then she leaped back into the tree.
She chattered at the two smaller squirrels.
Then one of them gathered up his courage
and jumped.

Oops! He missed!
Landing on the ground didn't seem to hurt
him much. He shook himself, ran back up the
tree, and tried again. This time he made it.
After he had eaten, he jumped back.
The mother squirrel chattered some more.
Then the other baby squirrel jumped.

His tiny paws grasped the edge of the pan
and he scrambled up. Soon he was eating away
like the others.
Davy smiled. "With all these mouths to
feed," he said happily, "I guess we'll just
have to get more birdseed."